NO CHEATING

AKASH MISHRA

"I would like to express my sincere gratitude to my amazing parents for their unwavering support and motivation in every situation life has presented me. I could not have achieved this without your constant encouragement and belief in me. Mom and Dad, your love and support mean everything to me. Thank you for everything."

Mom and Dad, I love you.

Contents

Acknowledgements

I would like to express my heartfelt gratitude to everyone who supported me in bringing this book to reality.

First and foremost, I would like to thank myself for not giving up despite many problems. I would like to thank my family and friends for their constant support and suggestions, and I am grateful to have you in my life.

I would also like to thank my editor and proofreader, Afreen Nazeer, for your expert guidance. Your insight and suggestions helped shape this book into its best possible form. Your attention to details was invaluable and I am grateful for your contributions to the final product.

To all of you, thank you for your invaluable contributions to this book. I am deeply grateful for your help and support, and I couldn't have done it without you.

Prologue

Aryan, a well-known entrepreneur, enjoys a complete life with a stunning wife, Maya, a trusted friend, Tanmay, and success in his business ventures.

Despite starting off as a happily married couple, Aryan and Maya's life took a sudden and unfortunate turn, leading to the erosion of their love and the emergence of doubt in their relationship.

In this story, you will be taken on a captivating journey that explores how a seemingly minor misunderstanding and a breakdown in communication can profoundly alter a person's character and nature.

Throughout the narrative, you will experience a whirlwind of emotions including love, friendship, doubt, misunderstanding, hate, and above all, the burning desire for revenge.

At the heart of this narrative lies a small mistake, and as the story unfolds, it becomes clear that this mistake has the power to completely transform the lives of each and every character in this story.

1

Chapter 1

Aryan, an entrepreneur, owned a small restaurant and bar business and enjoyed living in his beach house. One day, Natasha, his former secretary, showed up at the restaurant to meet him, but the staff turned her away.

Natasha's stubbornness becomes apparent as she disregards all warnings and remains at a nearby hotel. She visits the restaurant every day, hoping to catch a glimpse of Aryan, but always leaves with an empty heart.

As Natasha was leaving, a group of studs began to harass her until Aryan intervened and took her to his house.

Natasha raised an eyebrow as she took in Aryan's small new house. "So, running a restaurant and living in a cozy little home was always your dream?" You're finally living your dream, but there's no one to share it with.

Aryan replied, "I made this choice for myself."

Natasha couldn't help but asked why Aryan had chosen to abandon his life, despite having everything he could have wanted.

Aryan turned around, clearly annoyed, and snapped, "It's too late now." It's best to get some sleep now and depart tomorrow.

When Aryan went to the guest room the next day, he found Natasha had already left. He left for the restaurant soon after. As soon as Aryan arrived, he saw Natasha working tirelessly alongside the staff. He guided her to a secluded spot and inquired, "Is everything okay?" If I recall correctly, I asked you to leave, didn't I?

Natasha's response was cool and collected. She explained that since she wasn't told where to go, she assumed it was back to work.

When leaving, Aryan questioned Natasha if she had quit the job.

Natasha paused and answered. Although delayed, you did get it right.

Your absence created a void that couldn't be filled. The projects were left unfinished, clients lost trust, and partnerships crumbled, leading to a mass exodus of employees. No one wants to work with Tanmay anymore.

You should return to the company, otherwise, there won't be anything left.

Having listened carefully, Aryan stated firmly that he was living his dream and had no desire to return to his previous life.

"If the company goes bankrupt," Natasha asked, "would you abandon your dream house and Maya?" The potential loss of your dream home would be an enormous blow to both you and the company.

Aryan spends the entire night at the beach with a drink, listening to the sound of the waves crashing against the shore, and reflecting on his past and present life.

2
Chapter 2

One month back,

The heavy rain caused a power outage late at night, leaving everything in pitch darkness. Aryan is waiting anxiously in the dark for his wife's arrival.

Two hours had passed when Maya finally returned to the bungalow, her footsteps echoing through the empty halls. The lights turned on suddenly, revealing Aryan's wife in a dishevelled state. Her lipstick was smudged, and there were bruises on her neck, along with fingerprints on her body and hands, showing that she may have been in a sexual encounter.

Aryan left her alone in the bungalow without uttering a single word. Aryan has been away from the bungalow for a few days now. Despite the maid's text informing him that Maya was unwell and needed to be admitted, Aryan chose to ignore it and returned to his work.

Later that night, Aryan returned home and sank into the plush living area couch instead of retiring to his room. As she noticed Aryan asleep in the frosty weather, Maya quickly covered him with her cozy blanket and sat down nearby to observe him.

The next day, Maya jolted awake, her senses immediately detecting the smell of smoke. In the garden, it drew her eyes to the bright red of a blanket engulfed in flames. Aryan's angry glare at it was the last thing she saw before he left.

Day and night, Aryan spends his time outside the bungalow, coming home only when Maya is already asleep. This became a habit until one day, Aryan returned home early and caught Tanmay and Maya in deep conversation, their heads bent close together.

Tanmay greeted Aryan and they left Maya behind to discuss the project.

Tanmay informed Aryan about their profitable partnership and scheduled a grand event before leaving. Aryan agreed to it. Aryan sets foot in the study room and gets engrossed in his pending task. Maya observes he is occupied and heads to her room to relax.

3

Chapter 3

Aryan arrived at the party preparation site the next day to help Tanmay. Aryan and his colleagues lounged comfortably, taking in the intricately designed event decor.

Tanmay takes breaks from work to say hi to guests at the door. Upon Maya's arrival, Aryan appeared perplexed and unsure of why she was there. Maya planned everything, from selecting the site to managing the event and decorating it. Tanmay revealed she was visiting to oversee the final preparations.

Maya received praise from everyone for her unwavering support, but Aryan remained oblivious and apathetic. Tanmay and Maya were busy with their pending tasks, so Aryan left with the rest of the crew.

When Aryan returned home late at night, the silence was palpable. He was just about to lock the gate, assuming Maya wasn't coming, when he saw Tanmay's car pull up.

As Tanmay and Maya stumbled around, Aryan took Maya's hand and praised Tanmay for making sure she got home safely.

Tanmay, who was inebriated, divulged that they had a great time after work and lost track of time.

Aryan walked Maya to her room in silence after Tanmay's departure. Aryan sits in the front chair, watching Maya's drunken state, and pondering who she's getting friendly with.

The next day, Maya woke up late with a pounding headache, but luckily, she found some medicine and a glass of juice near her to soothe the pain.

"So, did you get the medicine?" asked the maid inquisitively. "When I got to the mansion, everything had already been done," the maid explained.

In search of Aryan, Maya heads to the hall area, only to find a note informing her that he had left for a business meeting, and she has a meeting with a doctor.

Instead of going to the site, Aryan heads straight to his cabin at the company. He meticulously examines the pending projects, ensuring no detail goes unnoticed. Then, he calls the entire crew, including those who arrived late, to his office.

The sudden noise and cracking sound of breaking objects interrupted the meeting. They departed from the cabin and proceeded to pack their things. The other employees were intrigued by what had happened and started speculating.

Alisha, one of the project members, responded. Despite our almost completed project, we were fired without explanation and promptly dismissed.

Aryan comes out of the cabin and gives directions to the staff. You have a week to complete all your pending work, or you will be facing a massive layoff.

Tanmay, who was working at the site, hurriedly received the information and left for the company. When he arrived, he saw the crew working tirelessly until nightfall and ordered them all to go home. When he arrived at the Aryan cabin, he found the furniture overturned and shattered glass on the floor. Despite various efforts to reach out to Aryan, there was no response from him.

Aryan vanished for two days after giving a deadline, only to reappear unexpectedly at the site where Tanmay asked, "What's wrong with you?"

Maya appeared before the conversation started, asking Tanmay about the pending decoration, and then they both left Aryan alone.

Aryan sat silently among his colleagues, sipping his drink and quietly admiring his wife's diligent work. As everyone was leaving, Maya walked to Aryan's car and waited anxiously, but instead of Aryan, the driver appeared to take her home.

Tanmay apologized to Aryan before leaving, saying, "I know my behaviour was unacceptable and I'm sorry if I offended you. Please don't let my actions affect your relationship with Maya."

Aryan listens to Tanmay and said, "I understand. You've been friends since childhood, and she trusts you more than anyone else. Friendship is the most important thing to her."

Tanmay couldn't work peacefully the next day at the site, causing Maya to inquire about the issue.

Tanmay replied, "I think Aryan is not fond of our friendship and doesn't enjoy seeing us work together."

Maya reassures Tanmay that there is no reason to worry and takes his hand gently. Aryan passed by and noticed them getting close again, but he ignored them as he usually did.

Maya was leaving after Aryan departed, and Tanmay questioned if there was any issue between them.

Maya listened quietly to Tanmay's questions and left, saying nothing.

As Maya rests, Aryan stays in the hall area, staring at the door. It reminds him of the night when Maya arrived home in a miserable state, which showed that she had slept with a stranger. He feels annoyed as he wonders who the guy is with whom she cheated on him.

4

Chapter 4

Everyone had brought their families and friends to the company success party except Aryan, who arrived without his wife, leaving everyone surprised. Tanmay and his wife arrived at the party later, and one by one, the rest of the guests showed up. However, Maya was nowhere to be seen. A few guests questioned Aryan about the surprise he might plan, as they had never seen the couple apart before.

Maya arrived at the event after a while, wearing a beautiful well-wishing dress. Maya and Aryan stood side by side, silently waiting for the dance to begin, while other couples swayed to the music. Tanmay noticed Maya sitting alone and asked her to dance, which Aryan readily agreed to.

Aryan searched the eyes of everyone on the dance floor while Tanmay danced with Maya, trying to find any hint of a secret admirer, but found nothing. He excused himself to get more drinks.

When Aryan returned, the party was in full swing with loud music and people dancing. However, he felt bored and left without Maya.

At the parking, Aryan came to a sudden stop upon hearing Maya's voice and stood there, listening intently to her conversation with another person.

The stranger complimented her, saying she looked stunning in the dress he had given her.

"I wore it for you because I know it's the kind of thing you like," said Maya.

Stranger: I've noticed that you haven't been smiling much lately, and it's a shame because you look so pretty when you do. Is everything okay? Are you having any problems with Aryan?

Maya remained quiet for a moment before the stranger offered to take care of her like he did on a stormy night when she was alone.

"I don't want to repeat it again," Maya yelled, her voice echoing through the parking lot.

Stranger: I don't know you, but I want you to be happy, and I'm willing to do whatever it takes to make that happen, even if it means betraying my partner.

Aryan witnesses Tanmay and Maya kissing in front of him. Tanmay hid Maya behind him upon seeing Aryan and said, "We were planning to tell you everything, but it seems like we're too late?".

Aryan gazed at Maya, who avoided eye contact and confidently held Tanmay's hand without any shame. Aryan appeared devastated and departed silently.

5

Chapter 5

Maya returned home that night and found Aryan waiting for her. It was the same moment they had experienced before, but this time Aryan had many questions. However, Maya remained silent and was leaving quietly until Aryan asked if she had slept with Tanmay.

Maya appeared quiet, but her eyes spoke volumes. Aryan said, "I used to love you like crazy, but now you're dead to me. I released you from every bond we shared," and departed.

After three long days, Aryan finally returns home and collapses onto the couch in the living area. When he woke up the next day, he found himself wrapped in a warm blanket, feeling disoriented. He saw Maya sitting in front of him and asked, "Why haven't you left?"

"I needed to say goodbye," Maya replies softly.

Before leaving, Maya took a glance around the house. Aryan's watch alerted him to her high heart rate, so he caught her before she passed out and brought her to bed for some rest.

When Maya wakes up in her room, the doctor checks on her and Aryan asks, "what's up and if it's serious?"

The doctor replied calmly, stating that the cause of the fainting was weakness, and that rest was necessary.

Maya expressed her desire to leave after the doctor departed, but Aryan advised against it, saying that she needed to rest until she recovered.

"Did you decide to divorce me?" asked Maya.

Aryan stopped and said, "I already released you, but if it's important to you, I will ask the lawyer to prepare divorce papers. After you recover, we'll complete the formalities to release you permanently so that you can reunite with your partner without any obstacles."

When Aryan was away for a couple of days, Tanmay came to see Maya. When Aryan returned home at night, he saw them in the garden and made his way to the study room. Tanmay had left, and as Maya was making her way to her room, Aryan reminded her that he was the one in charge of the house and would decide who could come and go.

Maya clarified that the sole reason for Tanmay's presence was to monitor her health, since she could not leave until she had fully recuperated.

"I won't stand in your way if you need to leave," Aryan said, his tone firm. "But I can't have strangers coming in and out of my home."

"Remember, he's our friend and partner," Maya replied. Aryan didn't respond and left silently.

Tanmay and his lawyers were summoned to an urgent meeting to discuss a matter of great importance. Aryan arrived with his lawyer, and the meeting begun shortly thereafter. He suggested splitting everything equally, but Tanmay disagreed. Aryan stated that he no longer trusted Tanmay and wanted everything to be handled legally.

Tanmay's voice grew louder and more irritated as he spoke. "This company belongs to all of us, and we need to decide together."

If you insist on dividing everything, remember that I have a higher percentage of shares than you and showed Aryan the new chart.

Aryan was puzzled after seeing chart and asked, "If we have equal shares, then how can this be?"

"Maya had transferred all her shares to me, leaving you with only 30% of the company's shares." Tanmay revealed this news and put Aryan in a commanding position. "He gave Aryan a choice to either leave or continue with the partnership. If he left, Tanmay would file fraud charges against him, leaving him with nothing."

Both lawyers left, as there was nothing to change in the contract, and Aryan stayed silent. Tanmay stated he would meet Maya when it suited him since her house was part of the company, giving him all the decision-making power. Aryan decides not to go home that day and stays at the company.

The next day, as Aryan returned home, he noticed Tanmay's car parked in his garage. Upon entering his home, Aryan saw Tanmay walking out of Maya's room. After exchanging greetings with Aryan, Tanmay left.

Fed up with the situation, Aryan walked to his room and began packing his things. Aryan looked around the house one last time before leaving and left the keys on the desk. Maya inquired, "Have you ultimately decided to depart?"

"I lost everything already," Aryan replied with a heavy heart. "This house, which was once our dream, is the only thing I have left. But today, I learned how cruel people can be. If I stay here, I may die. It's better that I leave," he said before walking away.

6

Chapter 6

At present,

As Aryan entered his restaurant, he heard the chatter of the old company crew waiting. Aryan's frustration boiled over as he yelled at the staff, reiterating that he didn't want any uninvited guests lingering around the area.

Just as the staff was about to ask them to leave, Natasha stepped in and declared that they were there for their real boss and wouldn't leave until he was present.

Aryan, clearly irritated, grabbed Natasha's hand and forcefully led her out of the restaurant, causing the rest of the crew to quickly exit as well.

As the night wore on, Aryan found himself unable to sleep, and his thoughts turned to harming Natasha. He eventually left his beach house and stumbled upon a disoriented Natasha, who had been waiting for him all day.

Aryan led Natasha to his room, directing her to lie down on the bed. However, he was about to leave when she interrupted him and asked him to stay.

Aryan stays looking after her. Aryan's eyes roamed over Natasha's body, and he felt a surge of excitement. Natasha pressed herself tightly against Aryan, leaving no space between them, and Aryan's excitement grew even more as he gazed at her lips. He leaned in and kissed her, and she responded eagerly, feeling dizzy with desire.

Aryan suddenly regained his composure and quickly moved away from Natasha, getting out of the bed.

As Natasha woke up the next morning, she felt a stinging sensation on her lips and noticed a cut. She smiled as she watched Aryan diligently working with the staff. As Natasha was about to join Aryan, Tanmay stopped her and said, "You vanished. It seems like you want to abandon me. But don't forget, you signed the contract with the company."

As Tanmay reached out to hold Natasha's hand, Aryan unexpectedly interjected and grasped her hand, prompting Tanmay to intervene, resulting in a physical altercation and injury.

As the sun was setting, the police and lawyers arrived at Aryan's restaurant and placed him under arrest. Tanmay arrived at the jail. He saw Aryan behind bars and couldn't help but smile. "Look at you now," he said. "You were always a loser to me." With that, he turned and left.

Aryan was bailed out and couldn't help but wonder who had come to his rescue. As Aryan strode out of the police station, he caught sight of Maya, whom he ignored completely. He rushed over to Natasha and kissed her fiercely, leaving Maya standing there in shock.

At his beach house, Aryan continued to drink while Natasha sat bewildered, repeatedly urging him to stop and reminding him that he had already had too much.

Aryan dismisses her with a wave of her hand. "You can leave now. My intuition will guide me."

Natasha's voice quivered as she spoke, feeling trapped. "Do you want to get back at Maya? Is that why you kissed me? Or am I just nothing to you?" Despite my efforts to support and care for you, it's become clear that I cannot cure your heartlessness with love or compassion. Your burning hatred has consumed you, and only you can overcome it.

Aryan couldn't stop thinking about Natasha's words, even after she left. As he glanced at her company laptop, he noticed several upcoming projects that intrigued him. To get back at Tanmay, he composed an email to all employees and waited patiently.

The following day, a massive crowd from his previous company assembled at Aryan restaurant to celebrate. Meanwhile, Tanmay and Natasha, oblivious to the event, arrived at the office only to find it empty. Despite his many attempts to contact the staff, Tanmay could reach no one. He instructed his staff to locate the crew before the meeting began.

Natasha's phone beeped suddenly, and she saw a notification from one of her crew members who had posted a party picture on social media. Tanmay looked annoyed at the picture, so Natasha quickly hid the post and left.

Natasha left the company and went to Aryan restaurant, but it was empty, so she checked Aryan beach house. She found her laptop and quickly checked the sent invitation, realizing it was all part of a pre-planned trap. As she checked the details, she noticed the lively event taking place on the cruise ship.

Upon arriving at the spot, Natasha enters the ship and is greeted by the sight of the entire crew partying and dancing. She attempts to speak with some of them, but they are all too intoxicated to hold a conversation, consumed by drugs.

As Natasha tried calling Tanmay, Aryan snatched her phone, leaving her feeling helpless. She looked around for help, but no one seemed to care. She tried to flee, but Aryan locked her in a pitch-black room. Meanwhile, Tanmay was busy with a product launch where investors and media had already gathered at the company.

7

Chapter 7

Tanmay was alone and under pressure as the investors threatened legal action because of a missed deadline. Since Tanmay needed more time, they granted him a two-week extension to submit the product, or else the company and the CEO would face legal action.

As they departed, Tanmay turned to his men and inquired, "Did anyone else notice how everyone disappeared suddenly?"

Tanmay received a party invitation and immediately went to the ship, where he noticed the crew behaving strangely. Suddenly, a stranger appeared and injected him with a tranquilizer, causing him to collapse.

Tanmay woke up to find himself in police custody, charged with harassment by a female staff member. Despite Tanmay's claims of being invited to the location, the police found no evidence to support his alibi, as all proof had been erased. Tanmay was denied bail based on the evidence against him.

Tanmay's wife arrived later to help him, but unfortunately, it was too late. The incident gained widespread attention, and many people stood up against the company and its CEO. Tanmay was completely oblivious to what was happening to him and couldn't comprehend the sudden changes.

Tanmay had been in jail for three days with no legal representation until Aryan, who was warmly greeted by the police, arrived at the station. Aryan could meet with Tanmay separately. Aryan placed the evidence on one side and his demands for bail on the other. Silently, Tanmay took the list of demands and shake his head in refusal as he read through it.

Aryan's grip tightened on the Tanmay's neck as he asked, "Do you see any alternative to my proposal, given your stubbornness?"

Aryan advised him to consider his demands carefully or risk losing everything. If he refused, no lawyer would take his case, and he would be stuck there. If he agreed to split the shares evenly, they could both benefit.

With no alternative, Tanmay signed the contract with Aryan. Tanmay examined the evidence after signing, only to realize Aryan tricked him and left fuming after yelling at Aryan.

Aryan stands before his dream house, taking in the grandeur of its architecture. Aryan walks into the house and sinks into the soft cushions of the couch in the living area, waiting patiently for someone to arrive. Urvashi arrived as per Aryan's instructions, eager to do whatever it takes to secure Tanmay's release. She wasted no time in undressing.

As Urvashi started to remove her clothes, Aryan stepped forward to cover her, but she resisted. She asked him why he couldn't do what Tanmay had done with him.

Aryan seemed surprised when he heard this, and asked how she knew about it, since he had told no one. Did you tell anyone about this?

Urvashi empathizes with Aryan and questions his devotion to Maya, who betrayed him without a second thought. Despite Maya's hurtful actions, Aryan still cares for her deeply. Urvashi wonders why.

"Yes, I loved her like a madman," replied Aryan. "She cheated on me, but I won't sink to his level. I refuse to be like your worthless husband."

Urvashi held Aryan tightly and demanded an explanation, questioning why he had urged her to marry Tanmay despite knowing his true nature. She accused him of ruining her life and leaving her in a hopeless situation. Like a prostitute, I was ready to negotiate any terms that would secure my husband's bail.

Aryan's voice boomed as he confronted Urvashi, questioning her chosen identity. Even after all these years, you remain the same girl we met during graduation - kind and sincere. We both knew of your love for Tanmay and your request to marry my best friend.

"Will forgiveness be possible for what he did to you?" Urvashi asked.

Aryan remained quiet as Urvashi spoke. She went on to say that Tanmay wasn't the one for her, and that she felt safe with him. Urvashi held Aryan close and expressed her desire to care for him and heal his wounds.

Aryan declined her proposal, citing his friend's past actions as the reason for his reluctance. Witnessing Aryan's profound respect towards her, she felt grateful and apologized for her husband's actions before departing.

Aryan's sudden action left Urvashi breathless as he pulled her closer and began kissing her with desperation. Urvashi reciprocated his passion by clutching his hair and allowing him to kiss every inch of her body. Finally, Aryan pushed her onto the couch and climbed on top of her as Urvashi openly accepted his love, and they passionately made out.

As they were making out, Tanmay arrived unexpectedly, catching Urvashi and Aryan in a compromising position. In a fit of rage, Tanmay pulled out his gun and aimed it at Aryan. But before he could do anything, Maya appeared out of nowhere and shielded them. Seeing Maya, Tanmay lowered his gun.

With Aryan's bare chest exposed, he shoved Urvashi forward towards Tanmay and exclaimed, "We had a deal for your bail, and they've already released you before our agreement was completed."

Aryan interrupted Tanmay before he could speak and reminded him that the situation had changed. You once had the power to do as you pleased, but now the tables have turned, and I hold the reins.

Tanmay's tone was incredulous as he questioned, "You always treated Urvashi like your sister, so how could you?"

Aryan grabbed Tanmay's collar firmly and demanded an answer, "I treated you like a brother, but you not only deceived me in business, but also stole my wife and our company. You took everything from me through deceit."

Aryan released his grip on Tanmay's collar and disarmed him. He then reminded him of the power shift, as he now had control over Tanmay's wife, company, and business. Aryan declared that he had taken everything Tanmay once had in just one day, but he wasn't finished yet.

He aimed the gun at Tanmay and spoke, "Your life is all that's left. Make the most of it because when the time comes, I'll use your own gun to end your life. Consider this a loan, and I'll return it with interest soon." Asking this, Aryan skips the gun point from Tanmay and keeps the gun with himself.

Aryan remembered Tanmay's words and repeated them, "Now that I am in power, everything will be done according to me." He knew this meant he could visit Urvashi whenever he pleased.

As they departed, Maya turned to Aryan and inquired, "What did you do today? Can you bear the weight of their animosity?"

As soon as she finished speaking, Aryan angrily pointed his gun at her and warned her not to ever speak his name again. He vowed to make her suffer the same pain he had endured every day, promising that it would ultimately take her breath away. As for her lover Tanmay, Aryan vowed to destroy his present and future completely.

"You've already done your worst, what more could you possibly want from us?" Maya asked, her voice shaking with anger.

Aryan skipped the gun and held her closer, looking straight into her eyes. He admitted he had never looked into her eyes since he saw her with Tanmay, and although he tried to forgive her, he couldn't get over the image of Tanmay leaving their room. He vowed to make her suffer the same way he did and trapped her in the house, forbidding anyone from leaving or entering without his approval.

Maya left the room silently after Aryan's orders, and she could hear his warning echoing in her head. His words made her shiver with fear, and she knew Aryan would stop at nothing to make her life a living hell.

Aryan locked the door of his house, leaving Maya trapped inside, as he departed for his beach house.

8

Chapter 8

Aryan was welcomed back to the office with balloons, confetti, and a cake. When Tanmay visited the company later, he was surprised to see everyone busy cheering and planning for the grand event. He ordered everyone to stop and get back to work, but Aryan refused and encouraged them to continue.

Tanmay entered Aryan's cabin and was immediately hit with the sound of giggling girls. He interrupted, to remind Aryan about their unfinished projects.

As Aryan continued to focus on his work, Tanmay's frustration grew as he reminded him of the consequences of not submitting the product on time.

"You are wrong," Aryan replied angrily. "They will file against the company and the CEO. As per the latest contract, I hold the maximum shares. But since you are the CEO of the company, whatever consequences follow will come under your name. So be prepared."

Tanmay's voice was filled with disbelief as he spoke. "We started this company together in a partnership, and now you want to bury it all alone? I won't let you do that."

"Then leave the company," Aryan said, "and I'll purchase the remaining shares."

Hearing the same words Tanmay had told Aryan earlier, he looked shocked and asked if Aryan was still seeking revenge. He reminded Aryan that he had already taken his wife and company and asked what else he wanted.

Aryan's response was full of venom as he accused Tanmay of cheating on him while he had been working tirelessly to take the company to the next level. He promised to make him pay by taking away everything he cherished and ending his life himself. Aryan warned him to brace himself, as this was only the beginning.

Tanmay called for help as he anxiously waited for assistance after Aryan left.

Maya arrived while everyone was busy preparing for the event. Tanmay warmly greeted her and introduced her to the staff, including the new crew, as Aryan's wife and the event organizer. As we all know, today's event is planned to be grand, and Maya's presence is essential to make it a success.

Aryan's annoyance was palpable when he saw Maya at the company, especially so close to Tanmay. He immediately ordered the event to be cancelled and retreated to his cabin.

Natasha walked to Aryan's cabin and found him glaring at Tanmay and Maya through the window. Aryan's anger grew as he watched Tanmay hold Maya by the waist, causing him to break things in the room. Despite Natasha's attempts to stop him, she ended up getting hurt.

Tanmay heard a loud noise coming from Aryan's cabin and ran to investigate. He found Natasha injured and was overcome with anger and the desire to attack Aryan, but Maya intervened and stopped him. Aryan silently left while Maya held onto Tanmay's hand.

Once Aryan had left, Tanmay assisted Natasha in standing up and inquired about her well-being.

Natasha wrenches her hands away from him, her heart pounding in her chest as she replies, "Everything was fine until you showed up. It seems like disaster follows you wherever you go, first with your friend, now with this company."

Natasha quietly approached Aryan's beach house, where he sat drinking alone. This time, she sat with him in silence. She waited for a while, and then abruptly asked if Tanmay was the person Maya had cheated with.

With tears in his eyes, Aryan stopped drinking and looked at Natasha. She could see the pain etched on his face as she held him tighter. Natasha led Aryan to the cozy bedroom where he held her closer while resting.

Natasha was familiar with Aryan's gentlemanly behaviour with women, and upon seeing him upset, she impulsively kissed him. Aryan responded in kind, and as Natasha continued to kiss him, she undressed herself and became naked. Aryan began to explore her body, but hesitated when he reached her lips. Natasha reassured him, saying, "let me take care of you."

With his hand on her waist, she allowed Aryan to take control and kiss her passionately, biting her lip along the way. As the kiss came to an end, Natasha held his face and looked deeply into his eyes before whispering, "I need you."

Aryan's craving for Natasha's body didn't cease, even after making out until dawn. Sensing his desire, Natasha took charge this time, and they continued making out until Aryan was completely satisfied.

In the afternoon, Natasha found herself in Aryan's arms, gazing into his eyes. He eventually fell into a peaceful sleep, and she kissed his forehead. However, when he murmured

Maya's name in his sleep, Natasha felt trapped and carefully slipped out of his embrace before leaving.

26

9

Chapter 9

Aryan woke up alone and stumbled to the mirror, only to see several love marks on his body. He remembered he had slept with Natasha the previous night and held his head, wondering what he had done.

Aryan was in a rush to leave for the company, but before he could meet Natasha, Riya, Maya's friend, stopped him. He greeted her warmly, and she revealed Maya's poor health. Aryan immediately rushed to his dream house. Upon entering, he found Maya lying miserable and held her tight to his heart, asking nothing. He called the doctor and refused to leave her side until the doctor arrived.

The doctor arrived and diagnosed Maya. Before leaving, the doctor consulted with Maya. Riya, who wanted to know what happened to Maya, joined them. However, the doctor left abruptly, stopping the discussion halfway.

When the doctor left, Riya turned to Aryan and asked about Maya's condition.

Aryan seemed lost in thought, so she repeated her question a few times before he finally spoke up and asked, "How do you know she's not okay?"

Riya said, "she received a text from Maya who wasn't able to connect with you and asked me to inform you. I rushed to the company and fortunately found you there; otherwise, anything could have happened."

Upon hearing this, Aryan immediately pulls Riya closer. In response, Riya reassures Aryan that everything will be okay, promising to stay by his side until the situation is resolved.

She kissed Aryan with desperation, and he reciprocated with equal passion. "I miss the way things used to be," Riya confessed, her heart aching for the touch of Aryan.

As Maya rested, Riya led Aryan to the other room, where they indulged in a passionate moment. Riya has taken up the responsibility of looking after Maya at Aryan's house during the day and provides care for Aryan's needs at night. Maya's health improved quickly, and now Riya must depart. As Riya was leaving, she gave Aryan a kiss and said she would eagerly wait for his call.

Aryan quietly walked into Maya's room and found her reading a book calmly. Upon seeing that she was doing well, he turned to leave. As he was leaving, Maya asked him if he still cared for her as he always had.

Aryan stopped abruptly and retorted, "At least I'm not as cruel as you are," before turning to leave.

10

Chapter 10

Aryan rushed to his farmhouse to meet his client for a party event and found Tanmay and his secretary Sanaya already there. Aryan's face twisted with annoyance as he saw Tanmay, and he didn't bother asking any questions before telling them to leave.

Sanaya explained that she couldn't afford the party, but he insisted on coming because of her. She hoped that he could help her surprise her parents on their anniversary.

As Tanmay noticed them talking, he made a hasty exit, leaving Aryan alone. Aryan walked away from Sanaya, trying to clear his mind. Suddenly, he felt her grasp him from behind and ask, "Are you still mad that I left without informing you?"

Aryan said nothing as Sanaya held him from behind and tenderly kissed his neck. She explained she had to leave urgently because her aunt had informed her that her parents were unwell, and there was no way she could bear to be away from him if it weren't for that reason.

She held Aryan tightly, feeling his warmth against her skin, and kissed him with desperation. "I can't believe I went without you for months. Now, more than ever, I need you."

Sanaya undressed herself, looking at her desire Aryan locked the door, and they made out.

Aryan agrees to the contract and efficiently handles all aspects of the project for Sanaya, keeping costs to a minimum. The crew finished their work ahead of schedule and now stood eagerly awaiting the guests. Sanaya implored Aryan to attend the party with her. Aryan arrived at the site and immediately spotted everyone gathered in one place - Sanaya with her parents, Natasha surrounded by the company crew, and in the corner, Riya with Maya, who had helped bring her to the event after Sanaya's invitation.

Everything seems fine until Urvashi arrived with Tanmay. Aryan's irritation vanished, and before Tanmay could say hello, he seized Urvashi's hand and asked her to dance. Tanmay couldn't take his eyes off them as they intertwined their bodies in a mesmerizing dance.

As the dance ended, Tanmay held Urvashi's hand, ready to leave. However, Sanaya insisted they stay until the event ends. and left to greet other guests, but Aryan, who wasn't done yet, vanished. Maya was feeling bored and decided to leave, but Tanmay asked her to drop him off. She initially ignored him, but eventually agreed when Urvashi insisted on joining them for the ride.

Maya takes one last glance at the backyard room before leaving, but her curiosity gets the better of her, and she walks closer. She peeks inside and discovers Aryan in a passionate make-out session with both Riya and Sanaya.

Witnessing the unexpected spectacle, she lost her balance, but Natasha steadied her until Maya abruptly withdrew her support and hurried away. Natasha was feeling uncomfortable with her behaviour, and as she turned to leave, an unsettling noise caught her attention. She cautiously peered into the room, only to be met with heart-wrenching disappointment. Despite this, she found herself unable to walk away from the scene.

Aryan was getting dressed after the session when he saw Natasha. She looked at him and said, "Finally, I know who you truly are. You're not the same Aryan that I gave my everything to. You're not the one I love." and left.

Maya was in a state of disbelief when she saw something that she couldn't accept. Just then, Tanmay visited her house, and she hugged him tightly. Tanmay noticed that Maya was shattered and wanted to comfort her by kissing her, but Maya pushed him away, saying, "You should leave. I can take care of myself."

Tanmay wanted to comfort her, but when he saw her stubbornness, he left her alone. Meanwhile, Aryan was at his beach house, sipping drinks and thinking about Maya's pain. She seemed broken when she saw him making out with her friend. However, Aryan felt calm and decided to celebrate more. He turned to the other side, where Riya and Sanaya were already waiting, and joined them.

11

Chapter 11

As Aryan arrived at the company the next day, he heard Tanmay's voice raised in anger and saw Sanaya's distressed expression. He briefly considered intervening but decided to head to his cabin. Natasha entered the cabin and began searching for a file, but before she could leave, Aryan closed the door. He took the file from her hand and walked closer to her, but instead of touching her, he admired her body, moving his hand an inch away from her skin. Natasha watched silently; her eyes filled with anger.

Natasha hadn't left Aryan's cabin in a while, and when Tanmay unlocked the door and saw them together, he silently motioned for Natasha to follow him. As she was leaving, Aryan grabbed her hand and insisted that she wasn't going anywhere until he was finished.

Tanmay stood up front and called out Aryan, who harassed the lady employee, asserting his authority as the CEO of the company.

Aryan skipped hold of Natasha's hand and continued, "No matter what I do, whether it's flirting or harassing the office girls, they say nothing. It's not because they're afraid of me, but they also enjoy it. You know that I'm always good with girls. Don't believe me? Just ask your wife and secretary," he whispered in Tanmay's ear.

Tanmay was holding his collar angrily, and Aryan responded by gripping his neck tightly. He warned Tanmay that any action he takes against him, or the company will result in the collapse of his career.

Tanmay's hand slipped off Aryan's shirt, and he glanced over at Natasha. She already knew why Aryan was acting that way and stood by him, so Tanmay left quietly.

When Tanmay left, Aryan remained irritated. He poured himself a glass of wine and said, "Fine, I'll raise your bonus. Enjoy."

Feeling trapped, Natasha took the drink from his hand and retorted, "You can't treat every girl the same just because of what your wife did to you. I'm not like her." With that, she left.

Natasha was walking home when Aryan abruptly stopped his car and forcefully pulled her inside before speeding off to his beach house. The moment Natasha entered the room, she felt an overwhelming urge to leave. However, Aryan had already locked the door and thrown away the keys. She struggled to free herself, but eventually gave in and sat down in silence.

Aryan sat in front of her for a while before getting up and heading to the kitchen. The sounds of sizzling and clanging could be heard as he cooked up a meal. He returned with a tray of dinner, but Natasha declined. Aryan also refused to eat without her. As the night progressed, Natasha and Aryan remained seated in front, both feeling dizzy but unwilling to give up. Aryan gazed into Natasha's eyes, able to sense her emotions, and admired her body, starting from her neck and slowly moving downward.

Overcome with emotion, Natasha throws herself at Aryan. On the bed, Aryan and Natasha share a deep, intimate moment as she selflessly cares for him. As dawn broke, Natasha made her way to the door, only to discover that it had never been locked. Aryan had used this trick to keep her close.

As Aryan rubbed the sleep from his eyes, Natasha pulled him close and whispered, "I'm still here," knowing he had been searching for her. Aryan sensed her presence and pulled her even closer, causing Natasha to feel conflicted about his actions. One moment, he craves her care, and the next, he appears to be a stranger with no regard for emotions and only desires women.

12

Chapter 12

The next morning, Aryan woke up alone and made his way to the hall area. Suddenly, he felt a pair of arms wrap around him from behind. It was Natasha asking, "Did you think I left?"

Aryan noticed Natasha was still at his place and took her to the dining table, where she had already prepared breakfast. He made her eat, refusing to eat himself. Natasha was touched by Aryan's care. She asked him to leave soon, lest they get late for the office.

"What if your boss orders you to take a day off?" Aryan smiled and replied.

Natasha's smile widened as she spoke. "Today's the last day for project submission. Let me give the project to Tanmay, and then we can spend the rest of the day as you'd like."

Aryan withdrew his hand and reminded her to get ready or risk being late for work.

Aryan turned, annoyed at the mention of Tanmay's name after Natasha left to get ready, but he quickly refocused his attention on the project at hand. However, his thoughts were interrupted by an urgent phone call, causing him to leave in a hurry without informing Natasha.

Natasha walked out and saw that Aryan had already left, which annoyed her slightly. However, she suppressed her anger and quickly left for the company, realizing that mentioning Tanmay's name could have provoked Aryan.

Upon arriving at the company, she headed straight for Tanmay's cabin, where the investors were eagerly waiting to hear about the project. However, when Natasha rummaged through her bag, she discovered that the project was nowhere to be found. Tanmay appeared petrified upon realizing that the project had failed again, knowing that the investors would not forgive this time. They shouted at him, cancelled the agreement, and warned Tanmay they'd take him to court for deceiving them twice.

Once the investors had departed, the silence in the room was deafening. Tanmay sat motionless in his chair while Natasha anxiously awaited his next move. However, he simply told her to leave. As Natasha was leaving, Tanmay warned her that the person she trusted was not the right friend for her and that she would end up alone.

Natasha left the cabin and sat down, pondering Tanmay's words before eventually heading to the beach house. Upon arriving, she searched high and low for her project, but it was nowhere to be found. She resigned herself to wait for Aryan's return, but he wouldn't come back until the next day. Natasha refused to give up and waited for three more days, but when Aryan failed to return, she resolved to meet him on her own.

As soon as Natasha reached Aryan's house, she barged into his room and found him taking care of Maya while she rested. In a fit of rage, Natasha grabbed Aryan's hand and dragged him outside the room, slamming the door shut behind them. She argued with Aryan, demanding to know why he always left her halfway and returned to Maya. Can you clarify what you want from us? Your actions are sending mixed signals - you hurt her on one hand, but on the other hand, you're extremely concerned about her well-being. Please tell us what you truly want.

As Natasha spoke, Aryan listened in silence before nuzzling her away. He clarified the house belonged to him and his wife, and he wouldn't hear a word against her or their home. All that mattered was being there for his wife in her time of need and, as a husband, he couldn't abandon her.

"Do I mean nothing to you?" asked Natasha calmly, her voice barely above a whisper.

Natasha slipped out of the house quietly, noticing Aryan's silence. Natasha hadn't been to the company for a few days until she walked straight to Tanmay's cabin. Tanmay was in a meeting with lawyers, discussing how to save the company from allegations made by a client. He had ordered everyone not to disturb them, but upon seeing Natasha's miserable condition, Tanmay ordered everyone to leave.

Without uttering a word, Natasha embraces Tanmay and sobs, admitting that he was right about Aryan. Tanmay sat calmly beside Natasha, offering her words of comfort. "It's a good thing you found out about him now, before it was too late," he said soothingly. "Everything will be alright."

After some time, Aryan arrives at the company and makes his way to his cabin. Suddenly, Sanaya walks in and begins discussing his work, causing Aryan to become suspicious and ask her why she has his work details.

Sanaya said nothing as Aryan gazed out of the cabin and spotted Natasha with Tanmay. He walked over to them, and

Tanmay, upon seeing Aryan, smiled and quipped, "Looks like I've taken another precious thing of yours. It's funny how you didn't value it when you had it, and now that I care for it, you hate me."

Aryan got all mad and said, "She's not an object."

Aryan was reaching for Natasha's hand when Tanmay cut in and said, "She's with me now. But if you want to shoot your shot, go for it. No harm in trying, right?"

Aryan felt betrayed when Natasha refused to support him. However, instead of feeling low, he laughed out loud and reminded Tanmay that he had warned him about making mistakes.

He dialled the client and put the phone on speaker. "The CEO has betrayed you," he said. "He sold the project to the rival party. I have proof, which I will share with you as a welcome gift."

"What can I do for you in exchange?" the client inquires.

"I want to destroy this company," Aryan replied, his voice cold and determined. "Do this for me, and I'll give you something Tanmay never could–the most advanced project you've ever seen, delivered in just two days. I've already sent you the project sample for review. Please hurry, as you only have 15 minutes to provide feedback before I sell the project to our rival company."

Tanmay burst into laughter as he replied, "Do you take me for a fool? You expect me to believe your bluff that this company is yours? I'll have you know that I'll decide around here."

Aryan shifted his gaze to the other side of the room, where the entire staff had gathered. He commended them for their hard work in taking the company to new heights but informed them that their time working under Tanmay was coming to an end. To secure their jobs, he offered them the opportunity to work with him instead. However, they had only 5 minutes to make their decision.

As Aryan spoke, many of the staff stood at the back, listening intently. However, Tanmay noticed that only a few staff members were standing with him. He yelled at everyone, questioning their loyalty to the CEO, who pays them. He threatened to decide in a moment to determine whether Aryan's accusations were true. Tanmay clarified he would tolerate no one who sided with Aryan after that.

Aryan was looking down at his phone when suddenly he received a notification. He looked up and fell silent. Tanmay noticed and burst out laughing, asking what happened to his plan of destroying everything.

Tanmay turned to the other staff and continued confidently, "I've told you before, he's just bluffing. He can't do anything to harm me or this company."

As Tanmay speaks, a sudden crash shatters the glass, making a jarring noise. Aryan grabs a rod on the other side and starts breaking things recklessly, not caring about the damage he's causing, even injuring himself.

Despite bleeding, Aryan raised his hand to put the phone on speaker, and the client's voice rang out, "We agree to your terms and will take on your project."

Everyone savoured the sound, but Aryan remained indifferent, asking, "What about my return gift for this project?"

The client responded, stating that legal action had already been taken and securities were enroute to the company. They promised that by the end of the day, the company would be destroyed.

Just as Aryan finished his call, police sirens blared in the distance. He quickly ordered everyone to leave while a few stubbornly remained. Eventually, Aryan made his way over to Tanmay and asked, "I destroyed everything, just like I promised. Your name, your career, and this company are all gone."

Aryan smiled as he repeated Tanmay's words back to him. "I now realize that I did this to you not out of revenge, but because I never liked you. I tolerated you because of my wife, whom you deceitfully took from me. But now, you are nothing but a zero."

Tanmay and Aryan got into a physical altercation, which was eventually broken up by the police and security. He was restrained, while Aryan's hand was bleeding as he asked Natasha to join him. Tanmay seemed uncontrollable and was about to attack Aryan with a pointed stuff, but Aryan quickly pulled out his gifted gun and shot him in the leg and then the arms.

As Tanmay cried out in agony, Aryan sat before him with his gun, threatening to take Natasha by force to be his queen.

Tanmay snatched the gun from the security and aimed it at Aryan, questioning him, "It can't be true, can it? I'm willing to kill you."

Tanmay was taken down when all the forces suddenly attacked him, and the police head walked over to Aryan, asking for a decision on whether to kill him or seek revenge.

Urvashi arrived just in time to stop Aryan from acting and pleaded, "Please don't do this. I'll do what you want. Just spare him."

Aryan struck a deal with Urvashi, asking for her in exchange for sparing his own.

Aryan's rage boiled over, and he grabbed the rod, using it to beat Tanmay relentlessly. Just as he was about to strike again, Natasha stepped in front of Tanmay, pleading for him to stop. "He's lost everything," she said. "What more do you want?"

Aryan's grip on the rod loosened as he pulled her closer and whispered, "I want you," before kissing her passionately.

Tanmay wanted to intervene, but he was powerless. Seeing Tanmay's helplessness, Aryan said, "I know how you feel. When you took Maya from me, I wanted to kill you. But today, I have everything I want, and you mean nothing to me. So, enjoy your time in prison."

When the police took Tanmay away, Aryan pushed Natasha away from him. He was angry and hurt. "I believed you, but you betrayed me too," he said. "Now I don't want you anymore. You're dead to me, like Maya."

Before leaving, Aryan apologized to Urvashi and took responsibility for her and Natasha's well-being. He invited them to live with him in his new house.

"If I'm dead to you, why do you still treat me with the same care as Maya?" Natasha inquired.

Aryan's response was fuelled by the painful memories of being betrayed by loved ones. He vowed to never forgive them and instead make them feel the same heartlessness he experienced. The pain of betrayal was worse than death, causing some to contemplate suicide. Aryan claimed ownership over them and their fate, determined to inflict the same suffering they caused him. Natasha wanted to reveal everything, but he listens nothing and left.

13

Chapter 13

After a few days,

Maya, Urvashi, and Natasha shared a home. Whenever Maya fell ill, Natasha was there to take care of her. One day, Aryan came to visit the house with a doctor, and he stayed until the doctor diagnosed Maya's illness. Aryan always left before anyone could ask about Maya's health, but one day, Natasha searched for Maya's medical records when Aryan wasn't home.

Natasha went to the doctor's office to inquire about Maya's condition but was denied any information without Aryan's consent. The doctor asked her to leave, but as the doctor was called away to an emergency case, Natasha took the opportunity to search for Maya's records and left with them.

While on her way to Aryan's house, Natasha was suddenly kidnapped, and in the dim light, she mistook her captor for Aryan. Just as she was about to kiss him, she saw he was Tanmay, and Natasha was terrified to see him. She asked him how he could roam freely when he was supposed to be in jail.

Tanmay replied, his eyes twinkling mischievously. "It's not important what happened. What's important is what's going to happen next. Care to guess? I'll take back everything he's taken from me, and it starts with you."

Tanmay smiled at the silent Natasha and said, "I don't take pleasure in hurting pretty girls like you, especially when you're already going through tough times." Despite thinking that Natasha had also betrayed him like Maya, he had no use for her, but he was determined to kill the man who had much to lose, including Natasha.

Natasha's voice trembled as she pleaded, "What do you want from me? I'll do anything to make this right."

"I want Aryan's life," said Tanmay, "but if you can give me his secret, I'll spare everyone and leave with what I need most."

"He doesn't have any secrets," Natasha stated skeptically.

Everyone in that house had a secret, Tanmay replied, and Maya and Aryan were no exceptions.

"I don't trust you," Natasha replied with a hint of suspicion in her voice.

Tanmay opens the gate for Natasha to escape, and as she was leaving, Tanmay told her that Aryan still cares for Maya's health, even though he hates her.

Natasha halted and turned to Tanmay when she heard his words. Seeing her confused, Tanmay explained that Aryan's hatred for Maya was just an illusion that everyone believed. Behind it, he hid a dark secret - he not only loved Maya intensely but also held a deep secret about her life.

"You're lying," Natasha replied, her voice shaking with anger. "He told me you're the person Maya cheated with, and that's why he's taking revenge on you."

"Don't forget about the other side," Tanmay reminded Natasha. He was afraid of what I might discover about Maya's secret if she left him, so he got rid of me.

Natasha's confusion was palpable, as Aryan always kept Maya's test results hidden. However, Tanmay's words seemed to strike a chord with her. "Help me get Aryan's secret project," Tanmay continued, "and I'll make sure everyone is spared. Deal?"

Without a word, Natasha departed from the scene. As soon as Natasha reached home, she locked the door and walked straight to her room. Just as she was about to read the test results, Tanmay's warning rang in her head - Aryan had threatened to kill anyone who tried to uncover Maya's secret.

As soon as Natasha reached home, she eagerly opened the test results and discovered that Maya's health had deteriorated significantly. However, because of her haste, she had only taken a few pages of the report with her, leaving the rest behind at the hospital. Natasha quietly tiptoed into Maya's room after hiding the test result. She sat down next to Maya, who was resting, and Maya immediately sensed her presence and woke up, asking if she needed something.

"Are you okay?" Natasha inquired. "If you need anything, just let me know." When asked, Maya confirmed she was feeling fine.

As Natasha cared for Maya, she casually inquired before leaving, "What does Aryan hold most dear?"

Natasha noticed Maya's silence and spoke up, mentioning that Aryan loves two names the most - Mayra and Abhimanyu. She added he would do anything for them, even die or kill blindly.

As Natasha left Maya to rest, she locked the door behind her and saw Aryan waiting outside. She was filled with fear, but Aryan noticed her tension and asked if she was okay, touching her forehead.

Natasha couldn't believe this and holds him tight. Aryan firmly pushed Natasha away and reminded her to always ask for permission before touching him.

Aryan took a few steps back before saying, "Leaving the premises without informing me is unacceptable. I make all the decisions here and have provided you with everything a girl could want. If there is something else you need, just tell me. But from now on, you cannot leave without letting me know."

Upon leaving, Natasha expressed her boredom by saying, "I feel bored here."

Aryan stopped and looked back while Natasha kept talking. "I know you didn't want to stay with us, but I can't bear not knowing how you're doing. We won't bother you if you don't want us to, but please let us at least see you to make sure you're okay. That's all we want."

Without uttering a word, Aryan listened and then quietly left. Aryan had left, and Natasha found herself alone with the keys that she had slyly taken from him. She tiptoed to the study room, which was strictly off-limits to everyone, and unlocked the door. As she stepped inside, she was greeted by the sight of countless books strewn around the room. Suddenly, she heard a noise and stamped out, only to see Urvashi resting in the hall. Natasha left the area without making a sound.

14

Chapter 14

As everyone was sitting casually the next day, Aryan showed up unexpectedly and announced, "Natasha and Urvashi, get ready to leave."

As they sat in the car, the silence was deafening. Once they arrived at the shopping centre, Aryan gave the girls free rein to shop. While Urvashi struggled to decide, Aryan stepped in and picked out a few dresses and jewellery for her. He even helped her try them on to make sure they matched. Urvashi was grateful for Aryan's help and happily agreed to whatever he chose for her.

As Aryan was preoccupied with Urvashi, Natasha searched for the items. Abruptly, she was tugged into the changing room where Tanmay demanded to know the progress.

Natasha's voice trembled with fear as she pleaded, "If he finds you here, he'll kill us both. You should go."

In a rush, Tanmay gave her a phone and warned her that if she didn't call him by midnight, he would come to her house to investigate.

Aryan was frightened when he couldn't locate Natasha. He searched for her, and she appeared, looking at a dress.

Aryan packed the dress and matching items before they left.

As soon as they arrived home, Urvashi asked Aryan if he could lend a hand with putting things away.

After finishing everything, Urvashi held Aryan's hand and asked him to stay a little longer to try out what she bought today.

As Urvashi tried on the dress and jewellery, Aryan patiently waited. When she finished, he began to leave. However, Urvashi slowly started undressing, and Aryan couldn't help but admire her body. Just as she was about to kiss him, he stopped her and confessed that he only thought of revenge whenever they were intimate.

Urvashi listened quietly before replying with gratitude. She didn't care about others' opinions but valued how she was treated respectfully, unlike her husband. Urvashi thanked Aryan for his kindness and showed concern for their well-being, despite any wrongdoing. She offered her care and support, hoping to ease any pain or loneliness they may be feeling.

Urvashi noticed Aryan's silence and crawled onto the bed beside him, searching his eyes for signs of loneliness. She kissed him passionately, offering herself to him in any way he desired.

Aryan gently lays her on the bed and instead of his usual wild approach, he softly kisses her forehead and apologizes for his mistreatment.

Aryan's slow and romantic gestures leave Urvashi feeling cared for, rather than used as a tool for revenge. As Aryan left Urvashi's room, he noticed that the study room door was unlocked. He searched his pockets for his keys, but they were missing. He remembered Natasha holding them on her last day and walked to her room.

As Aryan entered the room, he noticed Natasha lying alone on the bed, looking troubled. He walked over to the drawer and checked it but found nothing of interest. As he turned to leave, Natasha handed him the keys and looked annoyed. Suddenly, she pulled him back to the bed and tied his hands to the bedposts. Aryan looked even more annoyed, but before he could say anything, Natasha kissed him passionately, their breaths becoming heavy.

Natasha slowly undresses herself and unhooks Aryan's shirt, kissing him passionately while biting and licking. Aryan, seeing Natasha's wildness and stubbornness, forcefully unties one of his hands and holds her waist to pull her closer. He looks at the marks on her body and sees the desire in her eyes, realizing how much she misses his touch and doesn't want to hold back anymore.

Natasha's eyes locked onto his as she leaned in closer to his lips. "I may be upset with you, but I would never hurt you like Maya did," she said. "My feelings for you are pure, and if you can't reciprocate them, I understand. But please don't push me away like this. I don't have the same strength as you do, and I just need a little of care from you."

As soon as she finished, Aryan kissed her passionately, and they began to make love. Natasha held him tightly, and they continued until the break of dawn. Aryan took the keys from Natasha and cautioned her to never enter the study room without his approval.

Natasha had been searching for her things in the study room for days, but to no avail. Everything seemed fine until Urvashi called out for help while setting up her wardrobe, clutching her stomach in pain. Natasha and Maya rushed to her room to assist her. Aryan and the doctor arrived at the house later, and after diagnosing Urvashi, the doctor revealed that she was pregnant. Before anyone could react,

Sanaya arrived and hugged Aryan, excitedly exclaiming that he would soon be a father.

Aryan listened to two pieces of good news, and as Maya walked silently to her room, he held Urvashi and Sanaya, cautioning them to be more careful now that they had one more life to take care of, while promising to take care of all their needs.

Saying this, he dashes to the study room and slams the door shut, locking it behind him. Just as Natasha was about to reach out to Maya, her phone rang and Tanmay's voice filled her ear, "How's the plan going?".

Urvashi arrived abruptly and questioned whether her pregnancy was causing any distress to Aryan.

After disconnecting the call, Natasha comforted her and explained that the situation with Aryan and Maya was just weird, and that Maya was also involved. She reassured her that Aryan just needed some time and would eventually come to her.

Natasha walked to Maya's room and saw her sitting alone, staring at their couple portrait. She asked, "What happened between you guys that ended such a good relationship? Did Aryan do something wrong?"

Maya's voice rose as she defended Aryan, clarifying that their relationship was none of Natasha's business.

"If you still love him like crazy," Natasha asked, "then why did you betray his trust? Every day, I witnessed him slowly fading away, consumed by his love for you."

Maya replied, her words laced with bitterness. He thought he was hurting her by flirting with other girls and bringing them to her house, but it was he who was still wounded by the pain she had caused him.

Natasha's curse towards Maya was cold, as she accused her of being heartless. She questioned how Maya could reject the innocent man who still loved her deeply. Natasha then expressed her own willingness to give her entire life for Aryan's love. Though she acknowledged she could never replace Maya, she felt fortunate that Aryan still cared for her, even if only partially. Natasha wondered what would become of Maya, considering her actions.

The connection you once felt during lovemaking has been lost, and it's a curse you must carry until your last breath. I can't help but feel sorry for you and the choice you made because of Tanmay. Aryan had already ousted him and taken control of everything.

Upon hearing this, Maya asked what actions he took.

Natasha smiled, her eyes glinting with mischief, as she revealed the same gifted gun had almost killed him. But he had spared his life as a thank you for Urvashi's care. Now, he was confined to a dungeon with other criminals, where he belonged.

Hearing this, Maya's eyes widened in shock as she wondered what Aryan could have done in anger. She quickly made her way to the study room.

When Maya entered the dark room, she immediately saw Aryan sitting in the corner. As she walked towards him, tears filled his eyes. He asked her, "Do you see what you've done? You knew that we always wanted a child, and this entire situation could have been avoided if you hadn't betrayed my trust. You not only ruined our relationship, but you also took away the one thing that brings me true happiness. I die a little each day knowing that I may never be a father, and today, when I finally had that feeling, I feel no joy."

It's because of you I curse the day we met, and I can see that you're living a soulless life now. The Maya I once loved like crazy is not the same person before me. Now, I see an ordinary girl who betrayed me with my business partner and her best friend.

My children bring me a joy that you will never experience, and their upbringing will fulfil the dreams we once shared. As a good father, I will give them the love and guidance they need to thrive, while you look on with regret for what you've lost and can never regain.

15

Chapter 15

Aryan left Maya and the house, and there was a sense of emptiness in the air. Natasha's fear of Tanmay's presence and sudden calls has dissipated, and she no longer feels bothered by him. Aryan booked a routine health check-up for Urvashi and Sanaya on the same day. While Aryan accompanied Urvashi, Natasha took Sanaya to the hospital.

The sudden impact of the truck against Aryan's car left him bleeding and Urvashi in pain, but they managed to get out of the crashed vehicle. Aryan's eyes scanned the other car, and he saw it appeared to be in good condition, with Natasha and Sanaya safely buckled in.

Out of nowhere, Tanmay and a group of local hooligans surrounded the other car and Tanmay spoke up, "You took everything from me one day, and now it's my turn to take everything from you."

As Tanmay aimed the gun at Sanaya, Aryan stepped forward, willing to sacrifice himself if it meant saving everyone else.

Tanmay's eyes locked onto Urvashi's pregnant belly as he spoke, his voice full of anger and resentment. "What you took is unforgivable. I'll take something that you'll never get back, and then we'll be even."

Urvashi was saved from the bullet as Aryan shielded her, taking the hit himself. Tanmay, frustrated at missing his target, aimed his gun at Sanaya, but Aryan intervened before any harm could be done, resulting in a violent altercation between the two.

Aryan was outnumbered and alone, facing a group of hooligans led by Tanmay. Despite being badly hurt, Aryan refused to give in and continued to protect his family. As he slowly lost consciousness, he prayed for backup. Finally, the police arrived, and chaos erupted as both parties clashed.

As Tanmay took in the sight of Aryan's team, he realized they were much stronger than him. He tried to escape, but Aryan caught him. In a desperate attempt at revenge, Tanmay shot at Sanaya, but his aim was off. As the police approached, Tanmay shot Aryan again and fled, pushing Sanaya to the ground on his way out.

Aryan and his family were surrounded by police and guards, but unfortunately, they were taken to the hospital too late. At the hospital, Maya sees the miserable condition of everyone, which makes her feel broken. But when she enters Aryan's room and finds out he was shot, she sits next to him and holds his hand.

Maya was watching over Aryan late at night when she sensed someone approaching. She pulled out her gun and pointed it at the door, only to find Tanmay standing before her. He explained he needed to finish his work before leaving quietly.

While Maya was shielding Aryan, Natasha went to check his health and noticed Tanmay aiming a gun at Maya, causing her to freeze. Despite feeling weak, Maya still covers Aryan and questions Tanmay's actions, asking if what he's already done to them isn't enough. Tanmay replied, I am not leaving until I kill him.

Maya replied everything started because of her and asked to be killed for revenge.

Tanmay blamed everything on Maya, but what Aryan did to Tanmay cannot be forgiven, and he deserves to die. If you try to intervene, I'll have to forget that you were ever my friend.

Tanmay almost pulled the trigger when he saw Maya unmoved, but Natasha intervened with a pointed object. Despite being injured, Tanmay refrained from attacking her. Instead, he accidentally hit Maya while trying to attack unconscious Aryan. Tanmay then held Maya tightly to prevent her from bleeding until the police arrived and arrested him.

Maya, who was badly hurt, was supported by Natasha and yelled for help. While holding Natasha's hand, Maya said, "You need to know something before it's too late."

16

Chapter 16

After 22 hours,

Aryan woke up feeling dizzy and stumbled over to check on the two girls. He discovered they had lost his child, which caused him to lose control and start breaking things in a fit of rage. However, he suddenly remembered that there were other girls in the house and was leaving when Natasha arrived with blood on her hand. Seeing this, Aryan asked her what happened.

"Maya!" Natasha called out, pointing towards the ICU.

As Aryan entered the ICU room, he saw Maya lying on the hospital bed, struggling to breathe. He held her hand, trying to comfort her, and whispered, "Don't worry, Maya. I'm here with you, and everything will be okay."

Maya, despite being out of breath, skipped the oxygen mask and pleaded, "Will you forgive me?"

"I forgave you a long time ago," Aryan replied gently. "You're the most important thing to me."

Maya's voice was weak, but she mustered up the strength to ask Aryan if he would fulfil her last request, to which he agreed.

Maya handed Aryan a small box, and he opened it to reveal his wedding ring. As he slipped it onto her finger, he fulfilled her last wish of being his wife forevermore.

Maya's eyes filled with tears as she said, "I can finally rest in peace."

Aryan interrupts her, but she pleads for one last moment to feel his love.

Aryan's tear-filled eyes met hers as he kissed her lips, but he felt her body grow cold almost instantly. When he looked into her eyes, he realized she was no longer alive. Aryan let go of her hand and left silently, without taking a last look at her.

Natasha's heart shattered at the sight of Aryan, who refused to forgive Maya, yet he honoured her last request. She left Aryan behind and heard the rustle of clothing as he hastily dressed himself. Aryan left without shedding a tear.

As everyone gathered for Maya's funeral rituals, Tanmay was brought to the spot in handcuffs. He looked at Maya one last time and asked, "You promised you wouldn't leave me until the task was completed. Why did you lie?"

Aryan's confusion was evident in his tone as he asked about the plan.

Tanmay disclosed that she was carrying my child, but due to your interference, she abandoned us all.

Aryan replied, his voice filled with disbelief, "This can't be."

Tanmay's laughter echoed through the room as he exclaimed, "I may not have everything, but I have something even more valuable than what you possess: Maya's love. And in her final moments, she trusted me more than she ever trusted you."

Upon hearing this, Aryan wasted no time and shot him twice in the chest with the gifted gun, reminding him that he promised to kill him one day for his sin.

Tanmay's last words were a grateful thank you to his friend for bringing them together in the afterlife.

Aryan had his gun aimed at him, but Natasha appeared just in time and shielded Tanmay from him. She pleaded, "Don't do this. You'll regret it. Learn from your mistake and just let it go."

Aryan's rage consumed him, and he refused to hear anything, quickly pulling the trigger. Fortunately, Tanmay shielded Natasha and took the final blow. The sight of Aryan firing at Natasha left everyone stunned.

Aryan walked closer to Tanmay and knelt to be at eye level with him. He confessed he had suspected there was a connection between Tanmay and Natasha, but his doubts were put to rest when she nearly killed him in the hospital, and Tanmay didn't react.

She sustained injuries during the fight and was later found to have the same DNA as you.

Everyone was in disbelief after Tanmay disclosed that Natasha was his daughter. He had kept it a secret to protect her from any harm, but he realized that nobody could take better care of her than Aryan. I'm counting on you to take care of her, she's in your hands now.

Aryan withdrew her hand from Tanmay's and said, "I always treated you like a brother, but your greed has destroyed everything."

As Tanmay saw Natasha was safe, he breathed his last breath. The police consulted Aryan on the next steps.

Aryan held Tanmay's hand and made him hold the gifted gun, asking the police if it matched our plan.

The police responded, "Yes, we'll take care of the rest, don't worry."

17
Chapter 17

At the house,

As Aryan remained seated, the room was filled with a stunned silence upon discovering that he had already schemed to end Tanmay's life. Sanaya's voice was filled with sadness as she asked Aryan a question. "I thought life with you would be easier and beautiful, but nothing seems fine if I stay with you. I wanted to say a last goodbye." My child was a casualty in your revenge game, and I can no longer be with you.

Urvashi grasped Aryan's hand tightly after Sanaya had left. Her eyes filled with tears as she asked, "I know everyone makes mistakes and has to pay for their sins, but where did I go wrong in all of this?"

Your revenge game destroyed everything I held dear - my husband, my confidant, and even you, whom I hoped to heal with my love. But your hatred went too far, and you took the life of my child. I can't bear to be with a murderer any longer.

Aryan's voice was calm when he spoke to Natasha after the girls left. "You don't owe me any explanations, feel free to go."

"I can't leave you like this," Natasha replied, her voice laced with concern.

Aryan's voice was incredulous as he asked, "Even though I killed your father, you still want to live with a killer?"

"I was brought up in an orphanage," Natasha replied with a hint of sadness in her voice. "I don't know what it feels like to have a father."

Aryan's voice was laced with anger as he spoke, "I'm not the same person you once loved, no matter what you try. I'm even hating myself for what I've done to everyone."

Natasha pointed out that even though he despised everyone, fulfilling their last wishes showed that he still had a sense of compassion.

"You remind me of Maya," Aryan said before throwing her portrait. "I can't forgive her for what she did to me," he muttered.

"Are you the Aryan who would go to any extent for Mayra and Abhimanyu?" Natasha asked.

Aryan's eyes widened in surprise as he asked, "How did you know?"

In response, Natasha disclosed several things that were previously unknown and began to unravel the truth behind Maya's cheating.

Aryan was a caring and loving husband who fulfilled all the responsibilities of a noble husband. Their life was joyful until Maya fell ill. Aryan diagnosed her, treated her, and assured her that everything is alright. Following that day, he started distancing himself from Maya and flirting with other girls.

Maya often tries to win him back, and although he still cares for her, he avoids sharing the bed with her. Despite this, Maya remains optimistic, believing that one day he will return to her.

As Maya entered Aryan's office, she immediately noticed the unusual intimacy between him and Tanmay's secretary, Sanaya, causing her to leave abruptly. She reached out to Tanmay later and inquired about Aryan's secret, to which he initially denied but eventually divulged after taking an oath of friendship that Aryan has been unfaithful with multiple girls.

She learned this and left silently, waiting for Aryan to return home. As usual, he treated her the same way, and she believed he still cared for her. However, she sensed that he no longer wanted to share a bed with her.

Maya watched Aryan closely, waiting for him to share his secret, but he remained tight-lipped, leaving her in the dark. Every day, Maya's heart breaks as she believes her husband no longer needs her, but when he appears, she forgives him again and again.

One day, Maya went to Tanmay's house looking for Aryan, but he wasn't there. It started raining, and Maya was left alone with Tanmay who was a little drunk. Seeing Maya tense, Tanmay finally revealed his feelings for her and kissed her, which she refused. Despite Tanmay's efforts to make it up to her, Maya's condition seemed miserable, and she eventually secured herself and left.

When Maya returned home, she found Aryan waiting for her. He saw her miserable state and thought she had cheated on him. The deafening silence from Aryan killed their relationship that day. However, Maya didn't explain anything to him because she wanted him to feel the same pain she felt every day.

When Tanmay regained consciousness, he immediately remembered the pain he caused Maya and began visiting her regularly to apologize. Meanwhile, Aryan remained unaware of the situation and continued to accuse Maya of infidelity.

18

Chapter 18

At the company success party, everything changed when Tanmay demanded an apology from Maya in the parking lot. As Maya saw Aryan approaching, she pretended to kiss Tanmay, making it look like they had an affair. Aryan silently witnessed the scene and left.

Seeing Aryan's broken state, Maya felt a weight in her chest that made her want to collapse. Despite this, she held herself up.

Maya stops Tanmay before he could leave, reminding him of the night he nearly ruined their friendship and partnership. She asks him to pretend to be her boyfriend, explaining that it's the only way she can forgive him. Tanmay agrees, knowing that Maya's happiness is paramount.

Tanmay was so committed to playing Maya's boyfriend that he went to great lengths to make it real. He tricked her into signing over her company shares to him, effectively pushing Aryan out of her life.

Maya was aware of this and demanded Tanmay to give her the remaining share, threatening to sever ties with him if he didn't comply.

You sought revenge by sending Tanmay to jail, but your anger towards Maya, who betrayed you, led you to take everything from your friend. You took his company, his wife, and made Urvashi sleep with you. Although they falsely acted everything, but you still made them pay a high price.

Tanmay said to Maya, "Helping you is costing me too much. I might as well break this game or lose everything."

Maya swears they're friends for life, and Tanmay, who's crushing on her, puts up with everything Aryan does. But when he finds out Urvashi's carrying Aryan's baby, he loses it and wants to murder him.

Natasha was forced by Tanmay to retrieve Aryan's secret project, but Maya had already taken it. However, in her search, Natasha stumbled upon a file containing Maya's test results, which Aryan always dispose of, but had missed one in the study room.

Maya was devastated upon learning that she could never be a mother. She then read your diary, which you had always kept out of reach. Perhaps you were afraid of what she might discover. Upon reading your diary, she discovered you were flirting with multiple women, hoping to fulfil your mutual dream of having a child. You were dating women who might give birth to your baby in order to fill the void that would soon be present. Unfortunately, she was unaware of your intentions until it was too late, and Tanmay had already taken his revenge.

Maya was devastated after realizing that she was responsible for ruining everyone's lives, and even her fabricated story led to the deaths of two unborn children. She was so overwhelmed with guilt that she decided to end her own life. Despite needing medical treatment, she refused it and pretended to be in pain, hoping that death would come soon.

Aryan's anger erupted as he discovered the truth, and he threw objects towards Maya's portrait, shouting about her right to make decisions that impacted both of them.

Natasha held Aryan tight, trying to comfort him as he broke down. Aryan held up his empty hand and confessed that he had ruined everything out of hatred, believing that she had cheated on him. I had nothing to offer her, not even the baby she had always longed for, and she knew it too.

Natasha cuts him and says he still has one left.

Aryan appeared perplexed until Natasha placed his hand on her stomach and revealed, "I'm three months pregnant."

Aryan was curious and asked, "Did you share it with Maya? Did it bring a smile to her face?"

"Yes," Natasha replied with a smile. "Maya has already picked out names for the baby - Abhimanyu if it's a boy, Mayra if it's a girl."

Aryan held Natasha closer as he listened, tears finally streaming down his face after Maya's death, someone whom Natasha had cared for deeply, until he finally spilled out all his pent-up hatred. Natasha noticed Aryan appeared lost, grappling with the truth and unsure how to fix things now that he realized his perception of Maya and Tanmay was incorrect.

Natasha held Aryan's hand tightly and asked him to make things right by bringing back Urvashi, who suffered because of his hatred. Just like your friend, who went to great lengths to protect your wife, you too should take care of his wife, as they shared an unbreakable bond that withstood even the loss of everything they held dear.

"She'll never forgive me for what I did," Aryan said.

Urvashi's love for you is immense, Natasha replied. I've witnessed it firsthand and know that I can't love you in the same way. It's me who is urging you to bring her back, as no one else will care for her as you do.

Aryan asked before leaving, "Can you share my love?"

As Natasha smiled, Aryan turned and walked away.

When Urvashi arrived at Tanmay's home to pack and leave, she found Aryan waiting on the doorstep. He asked her if she would leave him like Maya did with no warning.

Urvashi controlled herself and replied, "You know I could never do to you what Maya did, but I can't stay with you any longer," as she prepared to leave.

He held onto her tightly, begging her not to leave and take away the joy she had brought into his life.

Urvashi's heart ached at the sight of Aryan's pain, and she instinctively wrapped her arms around him, declaring her unwavering love.

Saying this, she kissed Aryan, and they left.

After 3 years,

Aryan's dream of being a father is fulfilled now. He has three kids, Abhimanyu, Maya and Mayra. Abhimanyu with Natasha and the twins Maya and Mayra with Urvashi.

Aryan spent the evening with the kids, telling them bedtime stories until they drifted off to sleep. Afterwards, he checked on Urvashi and Natasha, who were also resting, before retiring to his study. As he gazed at the family portrait, he felt content seeing everyone together, including Maya and Tanmay. He then turned to Maya's portrait and reflected on how they had always wanted a big family, and now he finally had one.

THE END